I0520085

SHORT

and other selected short stories

By
Paul Holland

Copyright © 2010 by Paul Holland
All rights reserved.
No part of this book may be used or reproduced in any manner whatsoever without
the written permission of the publisher.
Published by SWG Marketing LLC, Little Falls, NJ
PAPERBACK ISBN 978-0-9722059-7-9

I would like to dedicate this book to all the people who read for the sheer joy of it...

Forward:

I think that the short story is a great vehicle for our times. After all we have created a culture that exists in the absence of time.

What better way then to enjoy and profit from the exercise of reading than to provide it in tiny bite size portions.

I hope you enjoy these eight little tales.

Paul

Table of Contents

The Meek Shall Inherit   1

Cheese   17

pH   27

Short   41

Bless You   53

Need   61

Ponzi   77

Mobius   89

The Meek Shall Inherit

He stared into those unreadable eyes, and swore he saw a bit of a smirk twitch at the corner of his mouth...but then I get ahead of myself.

The affair began three days into an idyllic sailing trip Roger and Rita had been discussing and planning for what seemed like an eternity. To date everything had run like a Swiss watch. The 32 foot Morgan sailboat they had hired through an Internet company had been sitting, fully provisioned and ready to cast off, even the rides to and from airports had gone seamlessly. The sun and wind cooperated fully and they had almost forgotten the day to day bedlam of the office which made the whole trip possible.

It was Rita who spotted the tiny island first, a few points off the starboard bow. As they closed the distance, they thought it might be fun to anchor, pack a picnic lunch and do a little exploring. The tiny strip of beach in the sheltered cove they found gave no indication that anyone had ever set foot upon it and after leaving a blanket and their cooler in the shade of a palm, they decided to follow a small stream that flowed from the interior. They were more than a little surprised when after about 15 minutes, they happened upon a small clearing that looked like a very well maintained farm, in direct contrast to the lush vegetation all around. There were several small buildings constructed in an ell that faced the precisely aligned fenced off planted sections on two sides. The meticulous rows of vegetables and fruit trees looked utterly out of place but the oddest sight were the dozen or so large white rabbits that lounged or hopped about the grounds. Although each area of the tiny farm was segregated by four foot high wire fencing, all of the gates lay wide open giving them free run of the place.

In the midst of it all stood a tall, thin, darkly tanned fellow about 50. His battered straw hat, dirty hands and knees instantly gave him away as the caretaker of this place. Roger waved and tried to address him in his best, broken Spanish only to be answered in a clipped British accent.

"Good afternoon, Can I help you? I'm sorry but I don't speak any Spanish, I'm afraid"

Roger stopped and a little at a loss for words started over, 'Yes, I'm sorry we thought the island was uninhabited. My wife and I were sailing, doing a little island hopping on vacation when we stumbled across your home here. We anchored in that little cove back there," he motioned back over his shoulder, "and were doing a little exploring when we discovered your farm here."

"Oh I see; you'll have to forgive me. Where are my manners? I suppose it comes from living here all alone for so long. My name is Creuthers. Please won't you allow me to offer you something cool to drink?"

Roger glanced quickly at Rita and replied, "Thank you, kind of you to offer. By the way my name is Roger Wilson and this is my wife, Rita. You say that you are alone on the island, Mr. Creuthers."

"Actually it's Dr. Creuthers and unless you count my friends here, we are quite alone." The older man gestured toward several of the rabbits that moved about freely as he led his guests toward his bungalow, "Together with another gentleman we built this facility to put into practice some of our research. Unfortunately my co-worker, a fellow named Wilcox passed away about 8 months ago."

Reaching the veranda, Roger and Rita settled into bent cane chairs while their host disappeared into the building. He reappeared a few moments later carrying a tray that held an icy pitcher and three glasses. After pouring out the fruity concoction, he handed a glass to each of his guests.

Rita remarked, "Oh this is delicious. What's in it?"

Creuthers turned to look at her and continued in his same unwavering monotone, "It is a blend of different fruits that I raise here. If you wish I can give you the recipe but part of the flavor I believe comes from the fact that the ingredients are so fresh."

Roger chimed in, "It really is wonderful. I've never tasted anything quite like it. I'm curious though, you mentioned that this was a research facility. If you don't mind my asking what kind of work are you doing?"

Almost mechanically Creuthers rotated to focus on Roger, "Plant genetics, specifically as it relates to nutrition which was a component of my old partner's field of study. I had developed a number of strains that provided a host of enhanced botanicals to promote brain activity. Our hope was to discover new ways to combat the onset of Alzheimer's and other similar degenerative mental disorders." Creuthers closed his eyes and shook his head quickly as if trying to rid himself of sleep and further collect his thoughts. He quickly opened his eyes and continued, "Forgive me, it has been such a long time since I have heard a human voice, even my own. It seems odd actually. One forgets living alone for so long."

A common pang of sympathy welled through the visitors as they watched their host refill their glasses.

"Please, it is already mid-afternoon. I would be most happy if you would dine with me before returning to your vessel. I suppose it is rather greedy on my part but I'd forgotten how pleasantly stimulating conversation can be. I hope you'll spare me a few hours."

Roger and Rita exchanged a look that expressed everything and she responded, "We'd be delighted Doctor, if you are certain it's not too much trouble. After all, our entire vacation is supposed to be an adventure. We aren't on any time table and your little retreat from the crazy, work-a-day world of cut throat competition is just lovely. Frankly, I envy your existence here puttering with your plants and tending your bunnies." She reached down and began stroking the large white rabbit that had taken up residence next to her chair.

Creuthers almost cracked a smile looking down at her new admirer lazing next to her. "Yes, these are New Zealand Whites. They are an excellent model of human physiology. That's why they have long been allies of medical and biological research." His face darkened, "Unfortunately that work usually resulted in pain and death for these gentle creatures. Our work has required none of that, in fact quite the opposite." The older man stopped himself and stood. "Why don't you amuse yourselves by strolling the grounds while I get cleaned up a tad and put dinner together? All I ask is that you don't disturb the natural flow here by interfering with the rabbits as the move about. Resist the temptation to feed or otherwise interact with them. Suffice to say it is very important to our work, I'll explain more at dinner if you are agreeable."

Roger and Rita nodded and watched as their host once more disappeared into the small bungalow, then got up and began to meander about the complex hand in hand drinking in the sunshine. The facility was much larger than they originally suspected. They did not find any more buildings but they did come across several more carefully cleared and tended gardens, laid out in the same fashion as the original except that there were no fences at all. After stumbling across the fourth such clearing, Roger stopped and looked puzzled. "I wonder how one man can manage to keep all of these gardens so neat. He must labor at it nonstop. With a jungle at its doorstep there's not a weed in sight. It must have something to do his plant genetics work. Hey, what if he's come up with a way to genetically prevent weeds from growing. Man, now that would be worth millions…"

Rita pursed her lips, "Maybe it is just a case of what you can accomplish when you don't spend your life tied to a cell phone, laptop and television..."

"Touché," Roger laughed, "You're probably right but still the anti-weed thing would be cool. Hey, do you think it's time to head back?"

"I suppose so. You know, I think I could get used to a lifestyle that doesn't include wristwatches."

They wound their way back down the path toward the compound and arrived to find their host waiting patiently. Showered, shaven and newly attired in khakis and a white short-sleeve shirt he now looked much more the part of a researcher or gentleman farmer. He moved as woodenly as ever but gestured to his guests directing them to a section of the veranda where a small buffet of food had been set out. The sight and aroma reminded Roger and Rita as to how hungry their day spent walking had made them. Their original lunch was still sitting in a cooler back on the beach after all and the prospect of dining on something that had not recently occupied a can was particularly attractive.

After they had all helped themselves, they once more settled back into the comfortable cane chairs that stood close at hand and breathed a contented sigh. Roger broke the silence, "Well Doctor if your research doesn't pan out you could always open a restaurant. I honestly don't recall ever having a better meal but I noticed that you didn't serve any meat. Are you a vegetarian?"

Creuthers nodded appreciatively, "Thank you – I'm glad you enjoyed everything. Eating vegetarian here on the island began as a convenience but I have found that I prefer it as a lifestyle. Everything you had today was grown right here."

Rita gestured toward one of the ever present rabbit population, "I see then you don't..."

"Oh heavens no," the Doctor continued, "Sadly researchers often conduct experiments which require that animals be subjected to invasive procedures, chemicals, diseases. The poor creatures are bled or sacrificed. Here our research evolved around behavioral studies. Seeing how our four legged research partners reacted to the nutritional benefits of various plant varieties we've developed."

Curious, Roger prompted his host, "Yes if you don't mind, you have made mention of your work to combat Alzheimer's and similar diseases. I'd love to hear more about it."

Rita echoed his question, "Oh and I would love to hear more of your views on the genetic engineering of plants. You hear so much in the media about Franken Food and other scare tactics. I mean, is it really safe, is it better? Obviously you are a proponent of it – it is your field. I'd just like to get your views."

Creuthers began, "Ladies first. Rita in answer to your question people eat genetically modified food every day. The overwhelming majority of food stuffs grown today exist as a result of human intervention. Classically, the creation of new strains was due to techniques such as grafting and cross-pollination. Technically, humans are still artificially influencing the outcome. Mother Nature herself is the consummate genetic engineer. One need only look at the incredible diversity of life to recognize that the Earth is her laboratory and all flora and fauna are part of her grand experiment."

Rita nodded in agreement, "But I think the problem derives from these extreme cases of gene splicing, you know where the DNA of an animal is incorporated into a plant, things like that."

"What most people fail to realize is that the genome of all living things is far more similar than dissimilar. You have about 75% of your DNA in common with a pumpkin for example. It stands to reason. After all, the basic functions of life are consistent, why then wouldn't the majority of your genetic material be? When it comes to a question of safe, which do you think is safer - food that has had a minor genetic alteration to make it unappealing to a particular insect, more disease resistant, less prone to rot or would you rather eat food that has been bathed in chemicals like pesticides and preservatives?"

"Yes, but what about the ethics of it all?" she asked.

"What is ethical about starvation? What is ethical about the chemical industry? Nature creates countless rearrangements of genetic material. We are merely expanding the breadth of the experiment. Who is to say that nature has not already tried variations we are dabbling with, or whether nature would not eventually get around to it?"

Roger broke in, "Some very compelling arguments but tell me more about this research you are doing, it sounds fascinating.'

"Certainly, it was actually Wilcox really who discovered that a particular class of plant sterols had extremely useful properties in the activation of certain areas of the hypothalamus. Interestingly though, the results he was seeing seemed to have a cascading effect in other regions. In my efforts to increase the ability of various plants to express larger quantities of these particular compounds, we discovered serendipitously that other naturally occurring agents within the plants were multiplying the effect. The decision was made to set up this facility to further our work for two reasons. We needed the space to allow the rabbits we were using as biological models to range free so that they could develop working territorial areas. All living creatures develop habits. In order to recognize deteriorative brain disorders, it was necessary to study the animals as they went about their daily routines unmolested. Obviously if they were locked away in laboratory cages that could never happen. In addition we felt it necessary to shield our work far from the prying eyes of others. You see our investigations had revealed a most astonishing side effect associated with long-term exposure to these agents but it was only after we had been here for two years that the full implications of our work became apparent."

Almost simultaneously Roger and Rita came to the realization that their host had stopped speaking some time before, however his explanation had continued on uninterrupted. Both of them found themselves staring at

Creuthers' lips which were no longer moving yet they were hearing every word.

The doctor, sensing their realization began to explain, "No you have not gone mad. You are simply feeling the effects of your dinner and that beverage you enjoyed this afternoon. The crops you see here about are all part of this grand experiment. We learned that the centers of the brain that were becoming active were enabling a form of mental telepathy, thought transference. Our work here rapidly shifted from a study of degenerative diseases of the brain to something far more elemental, communication."

"This is all very interesting doctor but it is getting late and I really think we should be going now." Roger nodded to Rita and both moved to stand up only to find that they were unable to.

"Please there is no need for alarm," the voice inside their heads continued. "You see based on your age and body weight, you have consumed enough of the plant complexes that it will permit you to act as receptors of thought transmissions. Your minds are new to all this and I realize it can be somewhat overwhelming."

For reasons he didn't clearly understand Roger asked, "Is that what happened to your partner, Wilcox? Was he overwhelmed?"

"Wilcox was complicated. His death was unfortunate and completely unnecessary. Against advice he attempted to leave the island alone, fracturing the mental bonds that had been forged. When he passed beyond the working limit of telepathy he went mad. He crashed the boat into a reef on the north side of the island and was drowned... very sad."

"Hah," Roger said, "That proves your story is bogus."

"How so?"

"If what you say is true then you should have gone crazy too as soon as Wilcox left because your bond would also be broken. I think you killed him for whatever reason, probably to take all the credit, money, power...and now you are going to kill us too."

"Oh good heavens, no. You have completely misread everything. Allow me to explain. It is really all about communication you see. Humans rose to the top of the food chain here on Earth but not because of opposable thumbs. It was because of their ability to communicate complex and abstract thoughts through language but language is still far from a perfect vehicle. That is why people are so often misunderstood, can't find the right words. Telepathy allows the complete and instantaneous transference of concepts without the filters and interpretation required by language. You are struggling with this because you are so new to it. You have been trained since birth to rely on the spoken and written word. These mental mechanisms that have been hard-wired with are battling with the more natural telepathic ones that you have just been introduced to. Over time with continued exposure to our native foods, your abilities and your reliance on them will increase but because you are developing so late in life you will always be much more limited, telepathically that is."

Rita sat frozen in her struggles trying to close out the thoughts that were intruding on her as Roger found the will to fight back one more time, "You seem to be doing pretty well, Doctor. Well if you can do it, so can we. We're not done yet. You can't get away with this."

What could only be described as a chuckle echoed silently through their heads, "Oh dear. I am sorry. You think that you've been conversing with Creuthers. Like you his abilities are severely limited. In order to truly develop one must be born and raised on this diet of food and mental exercise. I for example am fourth generation and allow me to say that we're glad you came and don't worry. You'll be well cared for."

In a sudden realization Roger stared down at the white rabbit that lounged comfortably at his feet. He stared into those unreadable eyes, and swore he saw a bit of a smirk twitch at the corner of his mouth…

Cheese

"It is utter nonsense of course." Malcolm mused while he savoring his cigar, "Still what an intriguing notion, the whole idea of capturing someone's soul."

Alan continued to study the chessboard and answered without looking up. "I suppose but of course that assumes you buy into the concept of having a soul in the first place."

"Oh that's right I forgot – you're an atheist, aren't you?"

Alan grimaced slightly, "Stop trying to distract me. I'm not an atheist. Frankly that would require far too much effort. I prefer to think that God and I have a gentleman's agreement, I won't believe in him if he doesn't believe in me."

Malcolm chuckled dryly and motioned for another dry sherry, "My goodness, you are a bit touchy this evening aren't you."

Sighing visibly, Alan looked up from studying the board. "I am merely trying to make you work for your victory here," he said gesturing toward the game in progress. They had been playing regularly for several weeks and it was all that Alan could do to make a game remotely challenging. Up until now he had always thought he was fairly adept at chess, but the old man was invincible. Still you don't get better by always playing people you can beat so Alan was willing to visit the club two or three times a week for a sound drubbing at his adversary's hands.

"Oh come now," Malcolm flashed a wry smile that seemed almost trademark, "you improve with every game and I enjoy our side conversations. They are always stimulating, besides it is checkmate in six moves anyway."

Alan sat back in his chair, "Well, I might have liked to play it out..." He knew better than to doubt his opponent's assessment and reluctantly turned his full attention to the subject of discussion. "So tell me, what is it that you find so fascinating about the prospect of stealing souls."

Having won both the game and his companion's full attention, Malcolm settled back as well and began to wax philosophical, "Throughout history and across cultures, the concept of a person's soul being tied to or captured by inanimate objects is the stuff of myth. Consider the ancient Egyptian practice of the elaborately carved sarcophagus. What purpose might it serve except as some form of conduit for their Ka, their soul?"

"There are any number of reasons that cultures would try to preserve likenesses in painting, sculpture, pottery... look at the thousands of terracotta solders found in China. Why can't it simply be art? Why this need to look any deeper?"

Malcolm was settling into his element, "What is art but an expression of the soul?"

"Perhaps it is just an occupation, a talent that has been turned into a profession. After all Michelangelo got paid, DaVinci got paid, Donatello got paid." Alan began to warm to the debate. Here at least he felt he stood a chance matching wits against the older man.

Malcolm's face expressed mock disbelief, "Surely sir, you are not saying that works such as Michelangelo's Pieta or Giotto's doors on the Baptistery of Il Duomo were anything less that acts of divine inspiration..."

Alan pressed his position, "If you or I were an artist living at the time we would be turning out works to please either a patron or the church, because they had all the money. I wonder how much of their inspiration was driven by the Lord and how much was driven by the landlord." He watched for a reaction, any chink in that smug armor that surrounded his opponent but if his barb had hit home Malcolm certainly wasn't showing any effect. The closest thing to an emotion that the old man ever seemed to display was mild amusement.

"Point taken. However we have moved far afield from the original topic. Can the soul be captured within an inanimate thing such as a statue, painting, photograph, etc?"

"I retreat to my earlier position, your question presumes the existence of the soul. Obviously if man has no soul, there is nothing to capture regardless of the means or method."

"Quite true, quite true... but if there exists a means to capture a soul, then the captured soul would itself be proof of it's own existence." Malcolm's enigmatic smile never faltered.

Alan snorted, "That is ridiculous. It is a chicken and egg argument."

"Not at all," Malcolm returned, "In science proof always follows conjecture. By the way the egg carrying the evolved genome would most certainly have come first, laid by some proto form of the chicken... but I digress."

Now it was Alan's turn to chuckle dryly, "We are not talking about science here. The entire notion barely rises to the level of theological mojo."

"Yet to quote the bard, there are more things in heaven and earth than are dreamt of in your philosophy, Horatio." Malcolm shivered slightly and as if on cue, one of the seemingly transparent staff silently stoked the massive fireplace burning nearby the old man. "Belief can be extraordinarily potent and manifest itself in a host of different ways that defy the explanations of mere science. Take for example things like fire walking and faith healing. Science endeavors to draw its own conclusions but still one must wonder."

"Wonder about what? That the mind is a powerful thing... That we can delude ourselves into believing almost anything and that the strength of that belief forms a self-fulfilling prophesy. Right now I believe that I'll have another whiskey." Alan waited a moment as the drink quietly materialized at his elbow. "Now was that caused by belief or merely the product of excellent and efficient service?" He raised his glass in a mock toast.

At that Malcolm's eyes narrowed almost unperceivably, "Oh I wouldn't say that. There are more than a few people I know who think that finding good help these days is nothing short of miraculous but once more we stray from the path. Given the assumption that man has a soul, how might one go about capturing it?"

"All right then, you win." Alan nodded, "For the sake of continuing our discussion, let us assume man has a soul. It would have to be an intangible thing, how could you hope to capture it by any tangible means?"

"I beg to differ," Malcolm replied warming to the challenge, "How else could one do it? Thoughts are intangible but we can write them down, we can dictate a recording of them. In the event that what we are trying to express is a difficult or complex concept that defies the vagaries and inadequacies of language, we might employ video, illustration, analogy...even, dare I say it - art."

"You just had to get that in, didn't you?" Alan smirked, "I suppose I had it coming. Still by definition all things tangible have limits. If souls are immortal, they have no limits. QED, they would defy capture."

"Ah yes, but aren't our souls bound within these fleshy shells we wear?" Malcolm gestured theatrically to his own rather bland, rotund bulk as it sat captive in his easy chair. "Certainly if these flawed, biological engines could house something so ethereal, there might be other means."

"Like marble in the hands of a master sculptor?"

"Precisely, my dear boy." Malcolm continued, "Consider Pygmalion, where the creator's love for his work causes life to be bestowed on that flawless stone or Wilde's <u>The Picture of Dorian Gray</u> where the man's hedonist debauchery is etched on his portrait rather than his body until the release of death."

Alan wagged a finger at his adversary, "Great fiction is still fiction. There have been countless stories of enchanted objects throughout history but they are only that, stories. Tales told around the fire to frighten the unwashed masses. Why not throw in a few witches, warlocks and werewolves while you are at it?"

"You make a sound point but the real question here is; does an event create the belief or does belief shape the event?" Malcolm paused a moment to permit the idea to sink in although he hardly expected a reply, then continued. "If the perceived victim of the magic truly believes their soul will be trapped, why couldn't it happen? Look at practitioners of sympathetic magic such as voodoo, the excesses of Hollywood not withstanding, they firmly believe in such things and can be profoundly affected by them."

"Really now, this is the 21st century..."

"Not everywhere. I believe that you mock the beliefs of others at your own risk. I'd like to share something with you." Malcolm produced a small ancient looking wooden box.

Alan exclaimed, "Good heavens, my grandfather had a camera just like that but I don't think even his was that old."

Malcolm ran his hand over the worn and stained wood that formed the box and looked up smiling, "Yes actually this comes with a fascinating story attached. It seems that a fellow sailing through the South Seas used this very camera to snap the picture of an old tribal chieftain and then proceeded to control the fellow by means of the picture which had captured his soul. As the story goes he managed to keep both the leader and his followers enthralled for many years."

Alan snorted, "Yet another unpleasant indictment of western culture but not entirely surprising, many primitive cultures place stock in such things. So what happened? How did the story end?"

"Well it seems that the old chief died rather unexpectedly in an accident. Naturally without him acting as an intermediary the rest of the tribe was suddenly freed from the influence of their self-imposed master. I understand he proved quite delicious. So I suppose in one sense at least, the story had a happy ending."

Alan sank back into his chair briefly and then stood up, "Malcolm you never cease to entertain. I suppose there is justice in this world after all and speaking of which I must get going. I have an early day in court tomorrow."

"Oh that's right you are prosecuting that fellow, Anders... the one who killed all those people."

"Tomorrow is just a motion hearing but yes I am. It is a very nasty business although I really can't discuss anything about the case, yet."

"Of course, naturally... I understand that completely." Malcolm purred, "I am certain when all is said and done you will regale me with all of the gory details. Until then I shall remain content to wait and keep the board set up. Hopefully you can find time to stop back later in the week."

Alan finished donning his overcoat, hat and gloves against the cold, "Well I'll do my best old boy, to keep the fire going."

"Oh I shall and Alan one more thing before you go..."

"Yes, what is it Malcolm?"

"Say *cheese*."

pH

"Would you mind terribly explaining why I have been dragged here against my will?" Wiley fumed, "I am engaged in some extremely important research, not to mention my other obligations to the university. This is nothing short of outrageous."

The figure across the conference table sat waiting until the scientist was finished ranting. In his neatly pressed coveralls and graying crew cut he looked like some comic book action figure come to life. "Dr. Wiley, I can assure that your presence here is absolutely necessary. If it were not, you would not be here. You may rest assured that as unhappy as you may be currently with this situation it pales in significance to the realities we are faced with. I apologize for any indignities you may have suffered in being brought here however with your help it is hoped that your stay with us will be as pleasant, as productive and as short as possible."

Wiley stiffened visibly. He straightened his tie and eyeglasses then smoothed back his hair. It was a routine of born of habit almost like taking a personal inventory. He performed these actions automatically, then having put himself back into order he responded. "Well would you at very least mind telling me why I have been brought here by your henchmen?"

"Forgive me. My name is Black and I am in charge of this facility. The precautions you were subjected to were dictated by the nature of the work we are conducting here and my henchmen as you call them are government agents. In that regard, that is all the explanation you should need at present."

Wiley returned the cold stare of his host for a moment, at least to the best of his abilities then said, half under his breath as he looked away, "Really, which government I wonder?"

Black stood up, straight as an arrow and towered over the now cringing professor. "Dr. Wiley, under the best of circumstances I doubt that I would ever be accused of having a sense of humor. Trust me, these are not the best of circumstances. Take a seat."

Wiley hurriedly found a chair not wishing to further antagonize his captor.

Black continued, "Please permit me to bring you up to speed. You are familiar with Dr. Randolph Stevenson, I believe."

"Yes, personally and professionally. We had both done some post-doc work at the same university."

"Your familiarity with his past work is part of the reason you are here. He was engaged is some top secret research at this facility up until 17 days ago."

Wiley interjected, "Forgive me but you refer to Randy in the past tense because..."

Black's mouth tightened, "Because he is dead." He waited a moment for his news to sink in before continuing. "He was killed in a laboratory accident in conjunction with his work here."

Wiley looked down at his hands. Obviously chemistry had its inherent risks but it was still profoundly disturbing. Randy was if anything exceedingly cautious. "How did it happen?"

"I will explain but in the interest of saving time I would like to do so on our way to the lab." As he spoke the big man stood up and motioned Wiley toward the door. Once outside in the corridor, he hustled the chemist into a waiting elevator and began a long and silent descent.

After what seemed like an eternity, Wiley summoned up the courage to speak. "I though you were going to brief me on the way."

With that the elevator reached its destination and the doors slid silently open to reveal a waiting golf cart in an expansive tunnel that vanished into the distance.

"That is my intention, but we have time. The lab is another mile and a half drive from this point." He handed the chemist a warm field jacket and pointed him toward their ride. Climbing behind the wheel he piloted the small vehicle down the tunnel toward their destination.

"Let me begin by explaining that while I am not ignorant of chemistry, I am not a chemist. I have sufficient working knowledge to manage this project. In that capacity, I will endeavor to answer all your questions. Dr. Stevenson was working to develop an incredibly potent new universal solvent. The need for this was driven by several other projects. Suffice to say that this had far reaching implications in other sensitive areas of research."

Wiley looked over at his stoic traveling companion, "Defense department research?"

"Be realistic Doctor. The military complex funds a host of different research in virtually every sector of science. Ironically, while it may not be their stated purpose or intent, the spinoffs of that work have benefited mankind immeasurably."

"Sure, you never know when you might need a better grenade." Wiley glanced over to meet Black's stony stare, "I'm sorry, please continue."

Black once more fixed his gaze on the tunnel ahead as they sped past crates, shelves and storage rooms on their descent. "It was 18 days ago that Stevenson announced he had made his breakthrough. He has synthesized a solvent that is simultaneously more potent that hydrofluoric acid or sodium hydroxide."

"That's impossible, it is fundamentally flawed. Acid and base behave completely differently. One contributes a hydrogen atom to a reaction – the other accepts one."

Black shook his head, "Wait, it gets more confusing. For some unknown reason it does not follow molarity as any chemical reaction must. Instead of being consumed in the reaction the solvent disrupts the chemical bonding of the material it is acting upon but without any seeming loss of efficacy. If anything its activity appears to increase. It is almost behaving more like a catalyst, but it does not merely alter the rate of a reaction – it initiates it. It defies logic."

Wily struggled to make sense of all this. "I need to get to the lab as soon as possible. I need to access his notebooks."

"That's a problem." Black responded, "When the incident transpired in the lab, it triggered an emergency system that flooded the space with liquid nitrogen."

"What!"

Black nodded, "The system was actually installed at the request of Stevenson. He wanted to have a failsafe method that could shut down the reaction on a molecular level."

Wiley stared at him in disbelief, "I could see that in a glove box containment, but the entire lab! That's insane."

Black stopped the cart and turned in the seat to face his accuser. "You fail to understand the magnitude of what has happened here. Stevenson designed the system. He knew exactly what would happen because he triggered it. Flooding the lab was an action of last resort. The solvent had already breeched two containment levels. Your friend gave his life to stop it."

"Oh my God," Wiley buried his head in his hands, "In light of all this I'm not certain what you expect me to do."

Black turned his face to the tunnel that still lead down toward the lab and restarted the cart. "I expect you to stop it. Ultrasonic readings of the ice block indicate that it is still slowly eating its way through. It is at 77° Kelvin and it is still actively working."

Wiley went pale, "Hurry."

When they arrived onsite, Wiley was able to view the carnage first hand while Black logged into a terminal to recall the last video surveillance camera clips just before the incident occurred along with whatever back up files existed. Twenty people had perished but that was nothing compared to the devastation that waited trapped along with them in that ice. The university professor turned unlikely hero listened intently as Black familiarized him with the equipment and systems. Crew quarters, supplies, everything he needed was here.

When the tour was finished Wiley turned to his guide and simply said, "Leave."

Black started to say something and thought better of it. Climbing back into the golf cart, he turned and headed back alone.

At 9 o'clock the next morning his phone rang. It was Wiley explaining that he would check in at least once daily if for no other reason so that they would know he was still alive. Other than that they should expect to hear nothing unless he had some special need.

At 3:34PM on Day 3, Black's phone rang.

"Black, Wiley here."

"Go ahead."

Wiley took a deep breath, his head was pounding from a combination of stress, fatigue and more caffeine than humans had any right to ingest. "Well the news isn't all bad – some of it is dreadful. Molecular activity persists despite near absolute zero conditions. Apparently, Stevenson's solvent is actually not only continuing at these temperatures, it is also increasing its activity level."

"How is that even possible?"

"I checked the figures several times hoping I was wrong because I could not believe it either but I think that I have unearthed the reason by piecing together some of Randy's notes. Stevenson's solvent is water."

Black felt as if his head would explode, "Water... how could water eat through glass. You saw the video footage. You saw what that stuff did to the lab and the people in it."

"Yes, I saw it." Wiley began again, "Let me explain. In a chemical reaction acids such hydrochloric HCl contribute their hydrogen, bases such as sodium hydroxide NaOH will break apart and contribute their hydroxyl. If they have the same molar concentration one neutralizes the other the sodium and chlorine combine to form NaCl, table salt. The hydrogen and hydroxyl ions combine to form water H2O."

Black broke in, "Thanks I took high school chemistry."

Wiley ignored both the interruption and the sarcasm and continued. "Because of its composition, water is the perfect solvent, one oxygen and two hydrogens. In nature the two hydrogen atoms bind to the oxygen of the water molecule and align at 104.5° to each other. This causes the resulting highly polar molecule to exhibit relatively powerful bonding with other water molecules using Van de Waals forces. That is why water has such a high surface tension. Water naturally undergoes a process of self ionization breaking apart into free hydrogen and hydroxyl ions but in low concentrations. Stevenson discovered a way to artificially alter the angularity of the hydrogen bond, effectively disrupting Van de Waals forces and dramatically altering the rate at which self ionization occurs."

Black stared at the bottle of spring water on the table in front of him. "What you are telling me is that we have turned the stuff that all life on earth depends on for survival into some incredible solvent."

"Actually it is worse than that." Wiley said matter of factly, "Stevenson managed to make water into the most powerful acid and the most powerful alkaline in the world, simultaneously. Having done that, rather than becoming neutralized in a reaction, it gradually converts existing water it contacts into the new modified energy state. In short it replicates itself. Don't ask me how. I have theorized that it has to do with catalyzing the natural action of self ionization. I believe that it achieves this by modifying the polar alignment of the oxygen atom's nucleus such that it will adopt the new configuration."

Ever the practical man, Black asked the next question, "What can we do?"

Wiley responded, "I believe that I might have a solution. I excised a tiny fragment of the ice block and using a plasma cutting torch that I found in a storeroom here, I fed the fragment through the inert gas stream directly through the plasma. At 30,000°F, anything passing through that stream should be completely broken apart and stripped of its electron shell. The resulting discharge was exhausted into a space I had flooded with liquid nitrogen. After the plasma discharge had an opportunity to recombine, condense and freeze I scanned the space for any activity of the solvent. It had been reduced by a factor of about 20,000. The agent was still present but dramatically reduced."

Black began to breathe again, "What are you proposing?"

"Well, you did say to call if I needed anything. We up the ante. The destruction of a material requires time, temperature and turbulence. I am going to need a small thermonuclear device, a few Kilotons should suffice. The explosion from such a bomb would be in a range of 10 to 15 million °F and that temperature would be sustained for a much extended period compared to my little plasma torch. I am hopeful that that will prove sufficient. Before detonation, you have to rig ewers of liquid nitrogen to blow and generate an ice plug in the upper corridor, just in case it does not manage to completely destroy the solvent. I will oversee all the installation. It is the best shot I can think of. Now you had better come get me, I have a few things to take care of quickly while you get what is needed in place."

Within 3 days, working around the clock everything had been collected and installed. Wiley had sent the technician crews back up while double and triple checking all of the final arrangements. Once he was certain that everything was ready he climbed into the golf cart and radioed Black. "Wiley here, everything is in place and ready to go."

Black started to say something when he heard the low level detonation. "Wiley, Wiley – what's going on – what happened – are you alright?"

Wiley's reply was cool and calm, "Why yes, everything is fine that was only the LN^2 being blown to set the ice plug."

"But you are still down there…"

Wiley continued, his voice had taken on a serene quality, "I know where I am and no, you cannot save me. The bomb is set to go off in 5 minutes giving the corridor above time to freeze over. You see Stevenson and I are the only ones who know how to make this doomsday solvent so I think I would do better to stay right here. I took the liberty of making certain all of Randy's notes were erased or destroyed topside. By the way if you look in the box labeled Backup Files, you'll find I left you a little something."

Before Black could speak Wiley switched off the radio. The tall man hurried down the hall to the small office the chemist had used to find the box he mentioned. It was sitting next to the desk where he had remembered seeing it, neatly labeled. When he tore it open however the box contained only two books, a copy of the bible and a book of poetry by Robert Frost. One of the pages had been bookmarked, it was a poem entitled <u>Fire and Ice</u>.

He felt the concussion under his feet.

Short

Walter Ferguson had heard all the jokes.

In fact he had been the brunt of them all his life. At 5'1" society had always treated him as if his height were a disability. It never mattered that he was intelligent, well spoken, efficient, industrious – in the condescending sight of humanity all that mattered was that "he was too fat to be a jockey and too short to be anything else". It was infuriating and the target of his silent wrath was his nemesis at the office, Anthony Greene. Tony as every called him was everything he was not. He was 6'3", athletic, handsome, a real charmer and dumber than a basket of turnips with the bright ones picked out. Walt hated him.

Throughout his 38 years he had suffered all the indignities that society could unjustly muster. He remembered going out on his first date in high school, only to be handed the children's menu in the restaurant. Even now there were stores which catered to "Big and Tall Men" while he would be directed to the boys department to find a suit. It was mortifying.

Now all that was about to change.

During the last month two events had driven things to a level beyond human endurance. First the always charming Tony Greene had been given the promotion... his promotion... the one he had worked for... slaved for... the one he had been promised. Once more the better man had been passed over to accommodate the taller one.

Then she had left. Sarah had not only quit her job at the firm, he found out when he tried calling her afterward that she had moved out of her apartment and had returned to the Midwest to live with her family. Walter knew why.

It had been the last straw and after a week of careful preparation at last everything was in place. Still he could not permit anyone to get a whiff of his plans. He smiled at his co-workers as he went about his business and for the first time in his life he spent his day anxiously watching the clock.

The next morning when Tony finally came to, every bone in his body hurt. He felt like he had been dragged under a bus. There was a nasty bump on the back of his head which was pounding and his mouth felt as dry as an old bone. He managed to force his eyes open and mercifully found his surroundings were dimly lit but he had absolutely no idea where he was or how he had gotten here. The light came from a small battery powered lantern that sat on the floor near by and he could hear the soft whirring of a small, distant fan moving a little air.

The room in which he was lying was tiny and perfectly round without windows or doors. The space was about six feet in diameter and the walls were at least twelve feet high. Everything appeared to be made of new concrete with the exception of the ceiling which was made of unpainted plywood sheets. In that otherwise unbroken ceiling he saw the outline of a small door that appeared to be the only way in or out.

Staggering to his feet, he managed to cry out, "Hey, what's going on here…" The pain in his head was excruciating. He had to stop and drop to his knees he felt so dizzy. Taking a quick inventory, he still had his wallet, keys and cash but his watch and cell phone were missing. He was trapped.

Eventually his head began to clear a little and he felt less dizzy but the thirst was killing him and he felt sick to his stomach. Once more he struggled to his feet and tried to call out. This time to his surprise the small door slid aside and bright sunlight poured in. Tony blinked against the sudden glare, "Hey who's there…get me out of here!" With the exertion, light and effort to yell his head once more felt like someone had driven a red hot spike through his brain.

Then a familiar voice said, "Oh good morning Tony, did you need something?"

"Walter, is that you? What kind of a stupid question is that? I'm in the bottom of a hole. Come on, help me get out of here."

Walter hadn't moved. "What's the problem? Can't you reach? Here try to jump up and catch my hand." He extended his arm down through the door.

Tony made the best effort he could but he could barely stand up let alone jump. Even at his best, he could not have managed to leap that high. "It's no good Walt, you have to get a rope or a ladder or something. Go get help... Wait do you have any water, I'm dying down here."

Walter stared down. "Gosh are you short on water? I'm sorry but I'm short too but I'll be back as soon as I can." With that he started to lower the door back in place.

"No wait, leave the door open."

Walter stopped and peered down again. "Sorry there is no way to prop it open but I'll be back."

Tony sat back in silence to wait for what seemed like an eternity.

By the time Walter returned the day had become sweltering, Tony felt a little feverish and when the door finally swung open once more he verbally lashed out at Walter. "What the hell took you so long? What are you stupid or something, I'm dying in here."

With that he trailed off into a string of profanity while Walter just smiled and said, "Oh I'm sorry – I thought you wanted me to help you..." and shut the door.

Tony was shocked into silence for about 30 seconds after which he launched into a tirade alternating between curses and sobs. After about 5 minutes, Walter reopened the door where upon the threats started anew. Walter smiled and began to silently close it once more as the trapped man's voice instantly changed to pleading and begging.

The still smiling Walter stopped and held the door open again. "Well that was fast…"

Tony was at his wits end, "What do you want from me? You… you put me in here didn't you?" He grimaced at the realization and the continued pounding in his head.

"Gosh Boss – it took you this long to figure it out. I imagine that is due to a combination of the side effects of the chloral hydrate, the bump on the head you got when I lowered you in and the dehydration. You might know the drug better by its nick name, a Mickey Finn. I probably gave you too much but I had to be certain it would knock you out completely. It was easy enough to accomplish. I know you keep a bottle in your desk drawer for a quick belt before heading out on Friday evening. All I had to do was wait until I was sure you had already taken a drink and then delay you with a plausible sounding excuse until it started to take effect. Since Monday is a holiday, everyone else had departed for the long weekend. I knew that you wouldn't be missed for 72 hours although frankly I find it difficult to conceive that anyone would ever miss you. At any rate, once you were unconscious, I used the company dolly and panel van to bring you here to the old family farm. We are out in the middle of nowhere – so go ahead and scream."

With that he slammed the door again and sat back down to revel in the sounds of despair for a while.

The next morning when Walter returned, his captive was sullen and quiet. He opened the door and looked down at the state of his former tormentor and rival. How things had changed. Tony had attempted to escape during the night by bracing his hands and feet against the opposing sides of his prison and climbing to the top. When he reached his goal he found that the door was latched tightly and having no way to brace himself, he could not force it open. In dropping back to the concrete floor he had badly wrenched his ankle preventing him from trying again.

"My, my, my – you don't look good."

Tony stared hollowly but refused to answer. His hatred was almost visceral.

Walter smiled coldly. "Try to look on the bright side, it shouldn't hurt too much longer at his rate."

"What is wrong with you... why are you doing this to me, you little monster?"

"Do you really want to know? You never cared before... In fact I don't think you ever cared about anything or anyone until now, except yourself but I'll tell you why anyway. It is because all my life I have been short. Not just in the physical sense but because of what life and people like you have handed me as a result. All my life people like you have cheated me, abused me, ridiculed me and why. Because they felt they could. Because of some genetic role of the dice you and people like you felt you were entitled to make me your whipping boy. Bet you don't feel that way now, do you?"

Tony shook his head, "You are doing this to me because kids in school picked on you for being short!"

"Yes and no. All my life I have been a convenient target for folks like you but you are far from blameless. In fact, I see you as the personification of all the miserable people that have persecuted and taken advantage of me. You stole clients from me, put your name on work I did to seize the credit, shifted blame to me for your screw-ups, you made me a laughing stock by lampooning me in front of the office staff and why? You weren't tall enough? You had to stand on my shoulders, to take what was rightfully mine."

"So that's it, I got that promotion because I deserved it. Not you, you twisted little refugee from munchkin land."

"Thank you for proving my point. There is equal opportunity as long as you are tall enough to go on this ride. You are a miserable excuse for a human being. I don't know what she ever saw in you."

Tony would have laughed if he could. "Oh so the truth comes out, you malignant dwarf. This is about Sarah isn't it... you liked her, didn't you."

Walter hardened. "She was a nice person. She was always kind and considerate but you didn't care. To you she was just another in a long line of bedroom conquests. You got her pregnant and tossed her off like an old shoe. Now she's gone."

Tony looked mildly shocked. "She was pregnant? She never said anything to me."

"Maybe she didn't think you'd listen."

Tony's speech was becoming more labored, "Look it doesn't matter. You can have her, I'll bow out. You can take my job, I'll quit the company…"

Walter looked down at him sitting, broken at the bottom of his makeshift prison. "You don't get it. The job is mine anyway, not that it matters as much anymore and as for Sarah – she isn't yours to give away. People are property and in another 24 hours, you won't even be people. You will just be a bad memory."

Tony pleaded, "Wait, you can't just leave me here to die."

"Tony, you have finally found out what it means to always come up short. Too short to climb out, short on air, short on food, short on water…SHORT, because for a change, you're down there and I'm up here. Good-bye." With that Walter let the door slam for the last time.

On Tuesday, people in the office wondered briefly why their new boss was absent but assumed he was probably sleeping off the excesses of a long weekend. After all that was standard practice for Tony. Then they proceeded with business as usual.

About 4 o'clock two gentlemen came in and asked to see Walter Ferguson. He invited them into his office but they asked him to accompany them downtown instead.

It seems that a local contractor had visited the farm looking for Mr. Ferguson. He had built a small silo for Walt just the week before from precast concrete pipe. In looking around in an effort to find the owner, he had climbed the ladder and peered inside, then he called the police. When they asked why he was on the property looking for Walter, he showed them the check he had been given. It had been returned by the bank. It seems the account was short of funds.

Bless You

"I assure you there was no reasonable means to foresee this outcome. All testing was conducted to the most rigorous standards."

Peabody was still trying to recover from his original shock in hearing the news. "Tell me, please Doctor, that you have something more than that."

"Well the fact of the matter is that we really don't fully understand the mechanism of the phenomena."

"Doctor Roi, that may very well be the single greatest understatement in the entire history of mankind. Jackson, how many doses of the antibiotic have been shipped to date?"

The small, thin man in the grey suit who had been sitting at the other end of the conference table thumbed through his notes quickly, "Just over 73 million sir, they have been distributed in all 50 states and three Canadian provinces. Inoculations have been ongoing for almost 5 months."

"Good Lord. Alright, we need to know what we are up against." Peabody resigned himself, "Doctor Roi, can you give us a complete download of everything we do know before the FDA arrives with torches and pitchforks."

Gupta Roi had been the lead researcher on the project and knew more about every aspect of development and testing of the vaccine that anyone. "The goal was simple; the road to get there was complex. The antibiotic sold under the trade name of Phagostat is in reality, a genetically modified bateriophage virus engineered to attack a broad range of super bacteria that have developed a resistance to traditional antibiotics. This methodology is not new having been used in the old Soviet Union and parts of Europe for over six decades. In this case we employed a method similar to gene therapy where we infect people with the cure. In short our mission was to use one class of pathogenic organism, the virus against another, bacteria."

Rather uncharacteristically the normally silent Jackson chimed in, "You mean like fighting fire with fire."

Doctor Roi looked over at the drab little man. "Well said, sir. There were a host of problems that existed in trying to create a viral magic bullet to combat bacterium. First among these was the solution had to attack a broad spectrum of bacteriological pathogens without doing harm to beneficial bacteria."

Peabody broke in, "Well that seems to be where the big problem came from, doesn't it. A little shortsighted I'd say, current counts list over 82,000 hospitalized or dead and the count is growing daily. Do you have any idea of the liabilities we are facing? People could go to jail over this one."

Doctor Roi's face flushed, "The cure was most effective, remarkable in fact and yes I am very aware of the ramifications of this anomaly. Fourteen members of my lab staff are dead, or worse. It was my understanding that the goal of this meeting was not to point fingers but to seek solutions."

Barely containing his anger Peabody nodded his agreement. "Very well, continue. Show me some way out of all this."

"To the best we have been able to determine to date, once in the general population, our bacteriophage LD97342 began to spontaneously mutate. It was a characteristic of adaptability we had inserted into the genome in order to provide it with broad spectrum properties. That is what helps it to perform so effectively."

Roi paused to take a drink, "The difficulty seems to have come from its association and combination with a rhinovirus strain existing in the general population and co-evolving. We do not fully understand the mechanism but somehow one serves to open the door for the other, it now migrates like the common cold."

"That's good. That could be very good." Peabody interjected, "If it is a free range mutation we could be off the hook."

Roi shook his head, "Our patented genetic material is integral to the new genome. We would have a very hard time distancing ourselves completely."

"Still it gives us some maneuvering room. Let that go for the time being. What do we know about this new virus?"

Roi bit his lip, "Well, from what we've been able to determine the chain of events occurred something like this. It seems to have first appeared on the 23rd of last month, it was a young man 18 years old in New Paltz, New York. He began exhibiting symptoms of a spongiform encephalopathy similar to kuru or Creutzfeldt–Jakob except that the disease progressed at an extraordinarily rapid rate and the normal mechanisms of transmission were absent. No one had any idea how he contracted the malady. He was dead within two weeks, but his mind was gone long before that. Autopsies showed that the destruction of his brain tissue was due to prion activity as expected but there was something different, something unexpected.

In looking at the endemic spread pattern the means of transmission mimic that of the common cold or flu. It is already rampant"

Roi paused a minute to retrieve a folder from his briefcase and placed it on the table in front of Peabody.

"Years ago, the World Health Organization in an effort to curb infant mortality in sub-Saharan Africa launched a massive campaign to inoculate children against the most common diseases. As a result, the infant mortality rate rose. Children stopped dying from the illnesses they had been vaccinated for, but what they didn't realize was that contracting and surviving those diseases gave them immunity to a host of other maladies. They were dying from everything else... I believe that the mutated phage is destroying a beneficial bacterium that somehow destroys or inhibits naturally occurring prion activity. In short I believe that our miracle cure for other diseases has become the agent that is destroying the cure that was protecting us from this more horrible malady."

Peabody sat nodding silently, "This may actually turn to our advantage. We have a head start. If we can cure this new disease it could be even bigger than Phageostat."

Roi looked at him in utter disbelief, "We helped cause this and all you are interested in is how to turn a profit from it."

"Doctor Roi," Peabody sternly returned the scientists stare, "we are in the business of curing disease. You said yourself that we didn't cause this. It was unforeseeable. We can fix this. People need us to fix it but there will be a cost no different than anything else we produce. Given the rate at which it is spreading we don't have a moment to lose."

Roi had to concede that regardless of how the business handled the rest, it was Peabody's last comment that rang true, they were racing the clock. Taking his leave, he retired to the main research facility located 14 miles outside the city. His entire team had taken up residence and worked 12 hour shifts around the clock. Time ran together as the reports of the disease reached pandemic proportion. On day 17, security called Roi to report to the front lobby where he found Peabody and a collection of 37 others.

The doctor looked at him incredulously, "Why are you here? This is a secure facility, we are working around the clock, and we don't have time for this. We must be left alone to work."

Peabody shut him down with a look, "These are members of the board of directors and their immediate family members. We are moving everyone of them in here for safety until you come up with a solution."

"I cannot have that. It will interfere with what we are doing. We are out of time already." Roi objected strenuously.

Peabody grabbed him by the arm and pulled him aside, "I don't care. These are the people you and I work for. They own this facility and you will accommodate them. You have absolutely no idea what is happening out there."

Both men whipped around at the noise.

"Bless you dear." She said as she handed the boy a tissue, "Remember to cover your nose and mouth."

Need

"There are people here, sir"

"People?" he looked up somewhat confused, "What people? I'm not expecting anyone."

"No sir," Krieger continued, "They are outside the gates."

"Outside the gates... what are they doing outside the gates? Where... on the road?"

"Actually they seem to be everywhere."

"You aren't making any sense at all Krieger. What do you mean everywhere?"

The security chief shrugged his shoulders. "I mean everywhere. There must be over a thousand of them. We got a call from each of the three gates saying that they were approaching. I personally checked with the remote video surveillance desk and they seem to be coming from every direction, surrounding the property,"

"Well, get rid of them. Isn't that what I pay you for?" He returned his attention to the report he had been reviewing.

Krieger remained standing there, "Well they haven't set foot on the compound yet sir. They aren't creating a disturbance. They are just standing around out there. Unless and until they enter the property or cause trouble technically we can't do anything."

His employer lowered the file once more and glared up at the man. "Must I do everything... then get the police out here. Need I remind you I come here, to get away from the noise, the news and the nitwits that consume my day? If you wish to remain in my employ I strongly suggest you exercise a little initiative and make this go away. So file a complaint. Use them for target practice for all I care, just take care of it."

Krieger nodded silently and retreated.

When he returned 3 hours later, lunch was being served pool side. "I'm sorry sir, but the problem is escalating dramatically."

"Didn't you call the police?"

"Yes, sir."

His voice dripped with sarcasm, "...and what did they say?"

"That is a big part of the problem, they didn't answer."

Krieger finally seemed to have his employer's attention, "What do you mean they didn't answer?"

"I mean that no one answered. They didn't answer their office line. They didn't even answer 911. Before you ask I already called the county and state. The good news is that they answered. The bad news is that they are so overloaded that they cannot respond. We are on our own. Based on that, I have taken steps."

"Do I want to know?"

Krieger nodded, "At this point I believe that you need to know sir. I called in satellite surveillance. We estimate that the crowd surrounding the property already number approximately 20,000 and more are flooding in."

"How is that possible... where are they coming from?"

"They are walking sir; it looks like from every direction."

"I don't understand, is this some kind of protest? Are they armed, dangerous? What do they want?"

Krieger shook his head, "As near as we can determine they are just unemployed and homeless. We have seen women, children and elderly mixed in their ranks. There is no evidence of violence but I have a call into the Governor's office to request the National Guard and I reached out to one of the security services companies we've used in the past. We currently have 38 of my own people here, pressing the entire household staff including your pilot and chauffer into service brings the total to 67 including myself but if trouble starts there is no way we could protect you for very long against a mob that size without more men. It's too dangerous to move you to the jet until we know if the airstrip has been compromised. We'll have additional men and material on site within 3 hours. We should be able to get you out then"

It was encouraging to see that his faith in his chief of security was not entirely misplaced but he didn't like the sound of *should*. "Good but that doesn't answer my earlier question. What do they want? Why are they here? Do they have someone in charge? If they do I want to speak with him, 5 minutes ago."

With his customary efficiency, Krieger responded, "Already working on it. Before coming here to report, I dispatched several of my people to grab a couple of them for questioning." Then he turned and moved quickly about the business of securing the grounds.

The total property covered almost 28 square miles, the majority of which was wilderness hunting preserve. There was a small air strip, golf course, lake, the house and all its attendant other buildings. He recognized that he first had to reduce his perimeter to the area immediately surrounding the main house. Fortunately his employer had always been a little paranoid, a professional hazard for a man of his wealth and position but it had insured that Krieger had the budget and discretion to take those measures he felt were necessary to protect the compound. As a result the surveillance systems were state of the art. He had a top notch arsenal at his disposal and enough ammunition to overthrow a third world country. Best of all his security team on site were all hand picked, battle hardened veterans. They knew their business and were used to taking and carrying out orders without question. On his way to the small detention room that had been hastily set up near the staff barracks, he systematically barked orders via radio to key positions. When he arrived at his destination he found his people waiting there holding a prisoner for him.

Calling over his two men before going in to the interrogation room Krieger said, "Fill me in."

Oliver, the older of the two men replied, "It's weird. It's like they're zombies that don't bite. We went out expecting trouble but they offered no resistance at all. We grabbed this guy, no one said a word. We told him to get in the Jeep; he just climbed in and sat quietly in the back. I'm telling you, it's freaky." His associate simply nodded his agreement silently.

Krieger pursed his lips, "What about weapons?"

Oliver shook his head, "Nothing, at least nothing that we could see. They weren't even carrying rocks and sticks. In fact from what I could see they weren't carrying anything except the clothes on their back. They must have camps buried back in the woods." If they did Krieger thought they're well hidden. They had not seen anything yet in their studies of the aerial views.

Krieger entered the small, Spartan room where their captive sat patiently at a metal table and closed the door behind him. "Thank you for taking our offer of hospitality, can I get you anything…water, something to eat?"

The ragged man who looked at least thirty pounds under weight for his height looked up, his hollow eyes saying more than his words, "No thank you. Was it an invitation on the part of your gunmen? Odd, it didn't seem that way at the time. They were rather insistent, but no matter."

"Why are you here?

The man simply kept staring at him, "Because we have to be somewhere."

Krieger hardened, "Don't get smart with me… just answer my question."

The man managed a sad, half smile, "I wouldn't dream of getting smart with you. I suppose we are here because Father John started walking and we started following him. Here we are. He didn't ask us to come, we just did. I suppose this is as good a place as any."

"This Father John, is he your leader? Where can I find him? Where is your base camp?"

"There is no camp, base or otherwise. If you want to find Father John he's right out there." the man gestured with one hand, "The last time I saw him he was close by where your men picked me up. If you ask people will direct you. Now if you don't mind I am a little tired." The man's chin sank to his chest and he thankfully closed his eyes.

Krieger re-emerged and pointing to the younger man told him to get their "guest" something to eat and drink, then he turned to Oliver, "I want you to get 6 men who are currently off shift and return to where you found this guy. You are looking for someone they call Father John. Get him and get him back here ASAP. Do not hurt him. Minimum force, understood?"

Oliver nodded, "Yes sir, Father John – minimum force, aye."

"Hey Krieger," a voice came from the room, "Looks like your guest is now an ex-guest. It seems he died in his sleep. What do you want us to do now?"

"Ah jeez," Krieger ran his hand through his hair, "Great I needed one more headache. Take the body with you. Dump it as close as you can to where you found him but don't let anybody see you and don't take any pains to disguise or hide it. They'll think he just keeled over. He wasn't exactly a healthy specimen. Next time I send you for someone to question try bringing me back one that isn't on death's door, okay."

"Only one problem with that, boss." Oliver quipped, "He was one of the healthier looking ones."

"Wonderful, and when you find Father John try hard not to break him...try real hard."

Krieger continued on with his methodical implementation and review of all his security procedures stopping first at the armory not only to issue instructions but also to supplement his own personal gear. He was normally in the habit of carrying two side arms, one primary and one concealed but this was obviously a case where he needed everyone in full tactical gear. He positioned four snipers and ordered the Gatling guns that overlooked each one of the three gates to go hot. When he was done he personally brought a flak jacket to his employer.

"Sir, just to bring you up to speed, we should be approximately an hour and a half from having our relief arrive. I cannot trust that the air strip hasn't been compromised with this small a force. We can't afford to move you yet on the off chance the crowd isn't harboring a stinger or similar weaponry. We took in one of their people who gave up their leader and my men have been dispatched to bring him in. At this time we are fully prepared and there has been no indication that a direct physical threat is imminent."

His employer glared back at him, "Of course, you mean except for that sea of humanity that is surrounding us."

Krieger in typical fashion retained his cool, professional composure. "Sir, you employ me to protect you. You are currently safe and secure. Given the situation, I'd say that I have been earning my pay."

With that Krieger's headset came alive and he tilted his head to listen. "My people are back in the compound with the mob's leader, the man they call Father John."

"Oh that's great; you mean they are a bunch religious fanatics...."

Krieger replied calmly, carefully measuring his words. "That is not what I mean. How many times have you see a political march lead by a minister? We don't know enough to leap to any conclusions yet. The good news is that we should know a whole lot more in just a few minutes and if we are holding their leader the likelihood of them trying anything stupid just plummeted. We were in good shape. Now we are in better shape."

"Tell your people I want him brought here to me, right now."

Krieger grimaced slightly and gave the order.

Approximately 10 minutes later, a man stood before them. It was an odd scene. Father John was painfully thin, unshaven, tottering on the brink of exhaustion and yet there was something about his eyes that stopped you. They seemed to look right through you to see something beyond, something you had missed. It was unsettling. Yet here he stood surrounded by this heavily armed militia in the midst of immeasurable opulence.

"Are you the man they call Father John?"

"That's what they call me, yes."

"Do you know who I am?"

"Yes, I have seen your picture before. I know who you are. They say you are one of the wealthiest men in the world. "

"The wealthiest and why are you on my property?"

Father John managed a thin smile, "Because your people grabbed me and dragged me in here..."

The man's eyes narrowed, "Mind you keep a civil tongue in your head, because I can have it removed if you don't..."

"I was merely endeavoring to be accurate." Father John's smile and soft spoken tone continued unabated, "I was not on your grounds when these gentlemen insisted I accompany them. In fact to my knowledge, no one with me was."

"My patience is wearing thin. What was your purpose in coming here?

"Although I greatly fear the answer will not make you very happy." Father John sighed, "Our purpose in coming here - was to come here."

"Stop playing with words and give me a straight answer."

Father John took a deep breath, "I will do my best to accommodate you. Stalin said that the death of a man is a tragedy; the death of a million is a statistic. Unlike the masses who seized the nobility during the French revolution and cut their heads off, these people have gathered in an effort to merely turn your head around so that you can see the misery your greed has wrought. They wanted you to stare into their faces and know who paid the price for your life of privilege."

Father John paused a moment as though slightly dizzy and then continued. "People wrongly assumed that they could put money to work. Money doesn't work, people work. Money cannot create anything or add value to something, people do. Money is only a tool, like a hammer – but if only a few people have all the hammers, no one else can drive nails. The economy everywhere has crashed under the strain. What little food there is cannot be had for any price. Fuel, infrastructure – everything is crumbling. I am certain you called the police, the military – they won't be coming. They have their hands full or they have already abandoned their weapons to join us except for a few renegade bands. There was no way to pay, feed or supply them either. So I hope you will train your cameras beyond the gates and survey your handiwork. I assure you that we mean you no physical harm, you may leave whenever you wish but I don't think that you will never be able to leave the ghosts of those souls out there behind."

Father John paused once more to compose himself, "Now if you don't mind I would very much like to rejoin my people. We have such a great many to bury and console."

The room was silent until he finally managed to shake off the spell of one tired old man's words.

"Mr. Krieger, take this fellow outside behind the cabana and shoot him. Tell Bradley to ready the helicopter, you can drop this man's body as a diversion while we take the jet and escape. I've give the pilot his destination once we are in the air. I want to be ready to leave in 10 minutes."

Krieger said nothing but turned soundlessly to the detail of men and motioned for them to escort the passive Father John, still smiling enigmatically from the room.

"Good, then you can report back to me when everything is ready."

Krieger did an about face and followed the others out.

Ten minutes later the radio came to life with Krieger's familiar voice. "Sir, Krieger here. Turn on monitor six; there is something you need to see."

Staring at the front gate monitor, he saw the man called Father John and 67 more people who had discarded their gear standing at the open portal. Krieger's voice once more came across the airways. "Sir, on behalf of the staff, we quit to the last man, including your pilots and driver. You employed me to keep you safe and I have always done just that and although you paid me it seems that I was incurring a debt without knowing it. I'm going now to spend whatever time I have left trying to pay some of that back. I hope it's enough. You can walk out whenever you wish. No one will harm you. So I guess I've done my job. Good bye and good luck."

With that he turned and walked with the rest of his fellow, former employees into the crush of humanity that stood just beyond the fences and vanished.

Ponzi

"Look, it's really simple I tell you. In fact it's foolproof." George took another deep pull at his beer mug.

Jim, who had heard this line more than once looked deservedly skeptical. "George, what the hell have you gotten into now? ...and why do you want to take me with you? Never mind, I know why you want me to go along but you can forget it. I'm not giving you a dime. I'm not buying any products, I'm not taking any subscriptions, and I'm not joining anything. You can keep whatever get rich quick scheme you are running this week and just keep running."

"Jimmy, you cut me to the quick. Look I know that some of the deals I have shown you in the past haven't worked out the way we'd hoped..."

Jim cut him short, "SOME, try all. If any of your instant wealth, just add money scams had ever worked out you wouldn't be sitting in this broken down gin mill trying to fleece me one more time. Forget it."

"Jim, Jim, Jim – hey I can't blame you for being mad at me but that's the point. I always got taken too. This time it's different. I've got it all figured out." George sported the most disturbing smile Jim had ever seen.

Jim motioned for Gina to bring two more drafts and said, "Okay you lunatic. Exactly what is it you have figured out?"

George chuckled, "It's brilliant. The reason we could never make it big in any of those pyramid things is that we were always the chumps at the bottom. We wound up paying in so somebody else got rich. The secret is that you have to be the guy at the top."

"Duh...that's your big secret. How do you plan on doing that, I'd like to know. What are you buying and selling that hasn't already been done? Even if you had something to sell, where are you going to come up with the money to get started and don't look at me."

"I got that all worked out, slick as a mink." George could barely contain himself now. "Just meet me here tomorrow night and I can spell out the whole deal for you. You still have your laptop computer, right?"

"Yes, and I am not hocking it or giving it to you. I need that for work." Jim started to bristle.

"Relax, Jim. I just want you to bring it so you can get on the Internet tomorrow so I can show you something, that's all."

Jim sat back in his seat and pushed his empty glass away waiting for his refill. "That better be all."

The next night as agreed, Jim walked into Flannigan's with his laptop case over his shoulder. Mike the bartender looked up and without saying a word directed him toward the back room. What greeted him was about as shocking as an ice cold shower. There stood George, at least it looked like George. He was as polished as a Wall Street banker. His suit looked like it cost more than Jim's car. In a word he looked the impeccable picture of success.

"Holy crow, George, look at you. Man you look like a million bucks."

"Jimmy, I'm telling you – if you want to make a million, you need to look like a million. Ahh, I'm glad you brought the laptop. Can you set it up and get on the Internet here?"

Jim couldn't get over the change. "Yeah, I'll fire it up." He set about starting and logging into the system. "I've got to tell you George – I just can't get over you, the change I mean."

"Thanks Jim, but wait. Before you know it you'll be tossing suits like this in Good Will because they got a spot on them. Are you on the Internet... here check this website out." George typed in a web address.

Jim was bowled over, nothing less. The website was state of the art. This looked like a billion dollar enterprise. "George, where did you ever come up with the money to create something like this? This is amazing."

"I got a guy, a college kid that owed me a favor. He's a real wizard with all this Internet stuff. I got him to create it."

Jim was left scratching his head, "Well I've got to hand it to you. You are knocking everything I'm throwing at you out of the park. Okay, what's the deal?"

George morphed into that same cat that ate the canary smile, "Oh Jimmy, you are going to love this. All these pyramid deals have to have an angle so here is how it works. You get ten people to sign up. Each one pays you $100 for the privilege. That's $1000, you pass $900 up line and you have already made your investment back. Each one of those ten, sign up ten more. That's $10,000 and they pass $9,000 up line, you keep 10% - that's $900. You have already made a 900% profit. Now, those one hundred people go out and find ten more each. The tier below you makes their $900 each but you get to keep 10% of the pass through. You get another $900. You just doubled your profit. But here's where it really gets good. By the time it gets to the time it gets to the 5th tier, you are a multimillionaire. By the time the pyramid gets to the 8th tier you will be worth over $6 Billion."

"Sounds great, and by the way how much prison time did Bernie Madoff get? This isn't just illegal, this is as illegal as it gets. Count me out. You can't do this."

George looked very disappointed at his old friend, "Jim, how come it's illegal to run numbers, unless you are the government. Then it is the state lottery. How come it is illegal for you to run a ponzi scheme unless you are the government, then it is social security. I told you I have an iron clad get out of jail free card on this one."

"Well if you do, you're the first."

George laughed, "Somebody has to be first, why not us for a change."

Jim shook his head slowly, "Well I'm here... go ahead, lay it on me. I have got to hear this one."

"Now that's the spirit Jimbo. The answer is simple. What is the one area where the government can't run roughshod over you?"

"I give up."

"The church of course, you dummy." George was grinning now from ear to ear. "As part of their buying in, each member – or convert if you prefer - signs an agreement stating their alliance to our new church, The Church of the Sacred Pyramid. Willing participation in our financing operations is just part of our faith."

Jim looked at him in utter disbelief, "You are totally out of your mind. Do honestly think that the law is going to sit still for this one just because we sing a few Alleluias?"

"I think they got no choice." George was rubbing his hands in glee, "Other churches support all kinds of internal charities, some even use gambling like raffles and bingo to raise money."

Jim was weakening, "There is a huge leap between buying a chance on a car or a bunch of old ladies yelling Bingo and what you are proposing here."

"No you only think there is. Look I already ran this past my cousin Bruce. He says we have a sound constitutional argument."

"Hold it right there, "Jim said, "Bruce, said that. Wasn't he disbarred for some mortgage thing a few years ago."

"That was all just a big misunderstanding." George responded defensively, "If that bimbo of a secretary hadn't ratted him out he would have had time to put the money back. He still knows the law and he says we are on solid ground."

Still unconvinced, Jim looked askance, "You are not filling me with confidence here..."

George held up his hands to quiet him, "Jim, let's talk reality here. If we do this you and I can be long gone with a whole mountain of cash while the attorneys are still habeasing their corpuses. Right?"

"Okay show me the rest..."

"This is really easy; every participant signs an agreement of allegiance becoming a member of our church in order to participate. We fill it full of all the usual religious mumbo jumbo, we pledge through all eternity, immortal soul, glory, glory, the whole nine yards. Then when they sign it, get this, they prick their thumb with one of those diabetic lancet things and put their thumb print on it."

Jim looked confused, "Why the heck do you want them to do that?"

"Three reasons. First, it visibly demonstrates their commitment to the faith. Second, legally try to argue that it isn't your signature. There is a fat chance of that happening. We have your fingerprint and DNA on record. It is the wonderful world of biometrics. Heck, a smart lawyer could tie this up for twenty years if he had to just on DNA evidence alone. Third and last, it is just really cool. The fact that our flock has that much skin (no pun intended) in the game will give the authorities second thoughts. What do you say?"

Jim thought for a minute, "You know this is just screwy enough that we might pull it off."

Through the weeks and months that followed Jim had to admit that George had been right on the money, it flowed in buckets. It seems that in addition to the cash, early people coming in were claiming status as ministers of their new religion and grabbing the tax breaks that went with it. George hadn't even thought of that angle but as soon as some enterprising soul brought that to the table, it encouraged whole new waves of "converts". In fact it took nearly 17 months before the first District Attorney started looking into their operation. It took another 3 months before they felt comfortable enough to rattle their sabers and demand the Church open their books. Of course by that time, money was no object and they were able to hire enough legal muscle to tie the courts up in knots for another 7 months. Of course all that time, the money kept rolling in.

Finally, the day came when Jim was hearing footsteps closing in behind him and he went in to see George. "Six more process servers hit us this morning. Between criminal and civil actions we are pretty much hitting critical mass. I don't know about you but I think retirement is calling."

George chuckled warmly. He was no longer the lean and hungry fellow who had first approached Jim with a crazy idea over two years before. He must have put on at least 40 pounds since then. "I think you are right Jim. It is getting to be that time. It has been one hell of a ride though. We've come a long way since the back room of that bar and grill, haven't we? As far as extradition goes, we could probably buy our own third world countries but then I've had my retirement mapped out since before that very first day. Tell me, what are you planning?"

Jim said, "I think warmer climates are calling. I have been slowly buying up acreage in a certain South American retreat. I took a page out of the drug cartel's book and in addition to establishing my own little fiefdom, I have gone out of my way to fund schools, orphanages, hospitals and the like. All good works for the church you know." Jim allowed himself a good laugh at the notion, "I've managed to become something of a local Robin Hood. The Feds couldn't pry me out of there with dynamite."

"Jim that sounds great." George said smiling. "We have Franklin and a couple of the second and third tier guys set up as sacrificial lambs.

Those prosecutions alone should keep the boys from the courthouse busy for quite a while."

"That's what I figure too. "Jim mused, "So what about you George? What do you have planned?"

"Oh I told you." George looked oddly serene. "I have had my exit planned since before you said yes. I have the perfect getaway, a place where the authorities can't touch me and there is my insurance policy."

George pointed at the rows and rows of filing cabinets containing registration forms.

Jim looked puzzled, "What is it? You have something on somebody big, don't you?"

George said softly, "Oh yeah, you can say that again. To date, we have collected over half a million of our special converts, the true believers. Jim, you look at that mountain of forms signed in blood over there and you see a flock of suckers at a few bucks a head, don't you."

"Of course, why wouldn't I? Are you telling me you see something different?"

"Sure I do, I see my retirement... my eternity insurance. Because they are all mine, even you."

In one swift calculated movement George's right hand appeared from beneath the desk and held the pistol pointing up below his own chin. The sudden noise and flash stunned Jim, freezing him in place. He stared, unable to look away from that awful scene as he felt his legs buckling beneath him. Dropping to his knees, gagging on the sight before him and the acrid smell of burning gunpowder that filled the room, he let his gaze wander back to all those cabinets...

Mobius

Vincent sat for a little while just catching his breath. "Phew, that was a good one. You know I always think that the third run of the day is the worst. Know what I mean... I don't know why I bother to ask you questions. You talk less than any man I know. Maybe that's why we are friends. You never talk and I can never seem to shut up. You know when I was a kid, my grandmother always used to say that I was vaccinated with a phonograph needle. I looked it up once. That was a kind of machine that they used years ago to play music and stuff. The needle would follow these grooves on a spinning flat disc and as it did it would cause a vibration that mimicked recorded sound. Then they would amplify it and boom – music, voice, whatever. Pretty primitive but it actually worked I hear. That's pretty funny, *I HEAR*, get it. Of course it wasn't as good as the digital stuff we have today, but it worked pretty well."

He stared at his silent running companion for a moment as though he might get a response although he knew he wouldn't before going off on another tangent...

"So anyway like I was saying yesterday I had this crazy idea... you know how when you are running sometimes you get these crazy ideas... anyway, I had this crazy idea about how all this got started. Well actually it ties in to a book on history I was reading. I know you are not a big fan of history but it is kind of cool sometimes to see how things were developed or how things came to be the way they are now... You know wars, politics, religion, social movements, inventions... It is all kind amazing I think. You know, what if we zigged here instead of zagged there? What might have changed, what would be different? It is kind of interesting to speculate sometimes, don't you think?"

Vincent sat for a moment extending the courtesy of waiting for a response he knew would never come, then he continued unabated, "For example, what if the old Soviet Union hadn't broken apart? What if the South won the civil war? What if Columbus never sailed? What if the British won the American Revolution? I mean history is full of *what ifs*. What if fire had never been invented or radio or steam engines or lasers or ball bearings? It boggles the mind, that little question what if. In fact, it makes you wonder about what you are doing right now and how will that affect what might happen in the future. I mean think about it. We work in a power plant, right? Who knows where the energy we generate here might wind up or what it might be used for. It could help some scientist in a lab somewhere cure a disease or electrocute some criminal or help some mom cook her kid breakfast.   Who the heck knows? Makes you feel kind of good about what we do for a living, like it is really important."

Once more Vincent paused, waiting for any acknowledgement at all.   When none was forth coming he shrugged his shoulders and merely went on undeterred.   "Which kind of bring me back full circle to how we got here.   Hey, that's pretty funny isn't it – full circle I mean... You know there is a thing call a mobius strip that is like a wheel where you could walk in a straight line along the inside of the wheel and wind up on the outside but if you keep walking you'll wind up on the inside again.   There are really pretty cool. Remind me later and I can show you a picture of one... Anyway, as I was saying about how we got here.   You know 2000 years ago they estimate there were only about 200 million people in the entire world.   In 1800 there were still only a Billion people and in 1900 about 1.6 Billion.   Then as medicine improved and there was more food, more energy – wham the population started to explode.   By 2000 you had 6 Billion people in the world.   But this is where my idea came from.   You see we keep getting more and more people but, we kept developing more and more innovation and automation.   We wound up with all these wonderful labor saving devices that suck up power, serving more and more people who are doing less and less.   It's all upside down and backwards. That's fine when you have lots of energy and only a few people but what happens when you have lots of people and not much energy? See what I mean? It only makes sense. So I figure working for the power plant we are pretty much set... By the way did you hear about Hank? I heard that he got shin splints."

For the first time Frank looked up at his co-worker as the buzzer sounded and the ready lights came on.

Vincent took a deep breath and started walking. His pace quickly became a jog, then a run as his giant wheel began to turn and gained speed. As the power meter on Vincent's unit registered a rate of 225 joules per hour his indicators went green. At that point, Frank's unit clicked off red and began to decelerate. As soon as it stopped the tired man stepped off and slumped down on the bench to catch his breath. As he sat and watched Vincent run, Frank thought Oh thank God – a whole hour of quiet.

About the author:

Paul Holland had the uncommon wisdom to marry his best friend over thirty years ago and together they managed to raise three fine young people.

The rest, is incidental.

Other books by Paul Holland include:

G
what if the gravitational constant, isn't (a novel)

Hobert does a Tradeshow
a modern business fable

Rocks in the Path
and a few other thoughts along the way

www.ingramcontent.com/pod-product-compliance
Lightning Source LLC
Chambersburg PA
CBHW071334130626
46556CB00004B/1890